Twilight Sparkle
Best Aunt Ever!

By Tallulah May
Illustrated by Zoe Persico

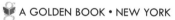

A GOLDEN BOOK • NEW YORK

Licensed by:

HASBRO and its logo, MY LITTLE PONY, and all related characters are trademarks of Hasbro
and are used with permission.
© 2017 Hasbro. All Rights Reserved.

Published in the United States by Golden Books, an imprint of Random House Children's Books,
a division of Penguin Random House LLC, 1745 Broadway, New York, NY 10019, and in Canada by
Penguin Random House Canada Limited, Toronto. Golden Books, A Golden Book, A Little Golden Book,
the G colophon, and the distinctive gold spine are registered trademarks of Penguin Random House LLC.

randomhousekids.com

ISBN 978-1-5247-6962-8 (trade) — ISBN 978-1-5247-6963-5 (ebook)

Printed in the United States of America

10 9 8 7 6 5 4 3 2

Keeping a baby Alicorn out of trouble is a **big** job. But Flurry Heart's aunt, Twilight Sparkle, has been a huge help! Princess Cadance and Shining Armor want to thank Twilight for everything she's done, so they decide to create **Auntie's Day**. They gather all of Twilight's friends at the Castle of Friendship to plan a surprise . . .

Party!!

Everypony has so many ideas. **Rarity** wants to decorate and make sure everything looks simply stunning for the party.

Applejack wants everypony to have enough to eat. "Apple pie, apple dumplings, applesauce, apple fritters, apple cake . . ."

Fluttershy has been teaching
her animal friends a song to sing.
They can perform it for Twilight.

Pinkie Pie thinks a party cannon will be
the perfect addition to the celebration—
along with streamers and balloons and
a dance party and presents!

But just as they finish planning, Twilight Sparkle walks in. "What are you all doing here?" she asks.

Rainbow Dash rushes over to distract her. "I need your help! With . . . the thing . . . in the place!"

Twilight is suspicious, but she follows Rainbow Dash back outside.

Rarity gets to work decorating. She thinks everything should be simple and elegant and purple, to match Twilight. But Pinkie Pie wants to help. More confetti! More streamers! More music!

Applejack goes home to her family farm, Sweet Apple Acres, to pick up some delicious treats while Fluttershy assembles her animal friends to practice their song.

Outside, Twilight is timing Rainbow Dash to see how fast she can fly.

"Are we finished yet?" Twilight Sparkle asks. "We've done this twelve times already."

Just then, Rainbow Dash sees Applejack inching toward them, pushing a huge pile of pies. Twilight is about to turn around and spoil the surprise, so Rainbow Dash waves her hooves in the air dramatically. "Oh no! I hurt my hoof when I landed. I need your help again!"

Applejack manages to sneak away.

Everything looks a bit . . . **bananas** in the Castle of Friendship. Decorations are hung from every corner. Fresh apple fritters are stacked high on every table. And the animal choir is trying to sing over the noise of Pinkie Pie's dance music.

"We need more space for food," Applejack insists.

"But where will we perform?" Fluttershy asks.

Ah . . . ah—CHOOO!

The decorations are destroyed. Fluttershy's animal friends have run away to hide. And there is applesauce covering every surface.

"Ruined!" Rarity exclaims.

"At least we still have the party cannon," Pinkie Pie says.

"I have a thought," says Princess Cadance. "If we put all your ideas together instead of trying to do everything separately, we'll be able to fix this before Twilight gets home."

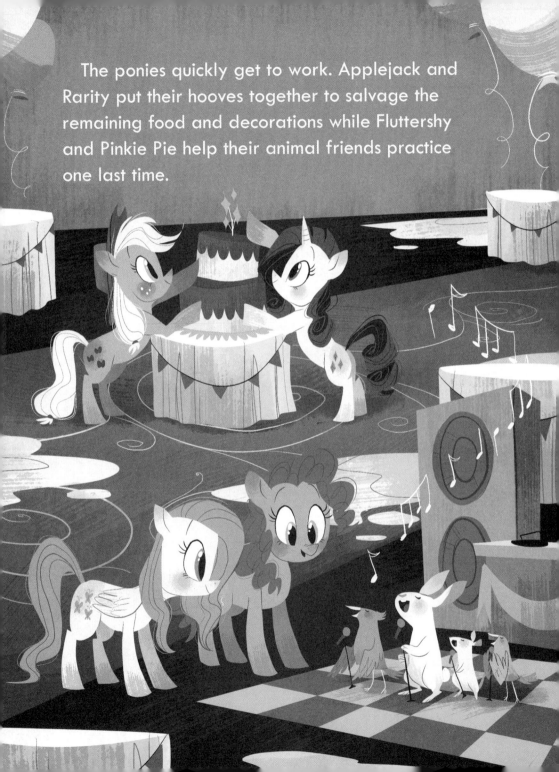

The ponies quickly get to work. Applejack and Rarity put their hooves together to salvage the remaining food and decorations while Fluttershy and Pinkie Pie help their animal friends practice one last time.

Everything is finally ready when they hear
Twilight's voice outside the door.

"I'm sorry you hurt your hoof, Rainbow Dash,
but the doctor said it was fine. Maybe you
should come inside and rest."

The door opens and . . .

"Happy Auntie's Day!"

Twilight is so surprised! She is delighted that all her friends have gathered together to celebrate. And she can't believe they managed to make everything look so perfect in only one day.

But then . . . Ah . . . ah—CHOOO!